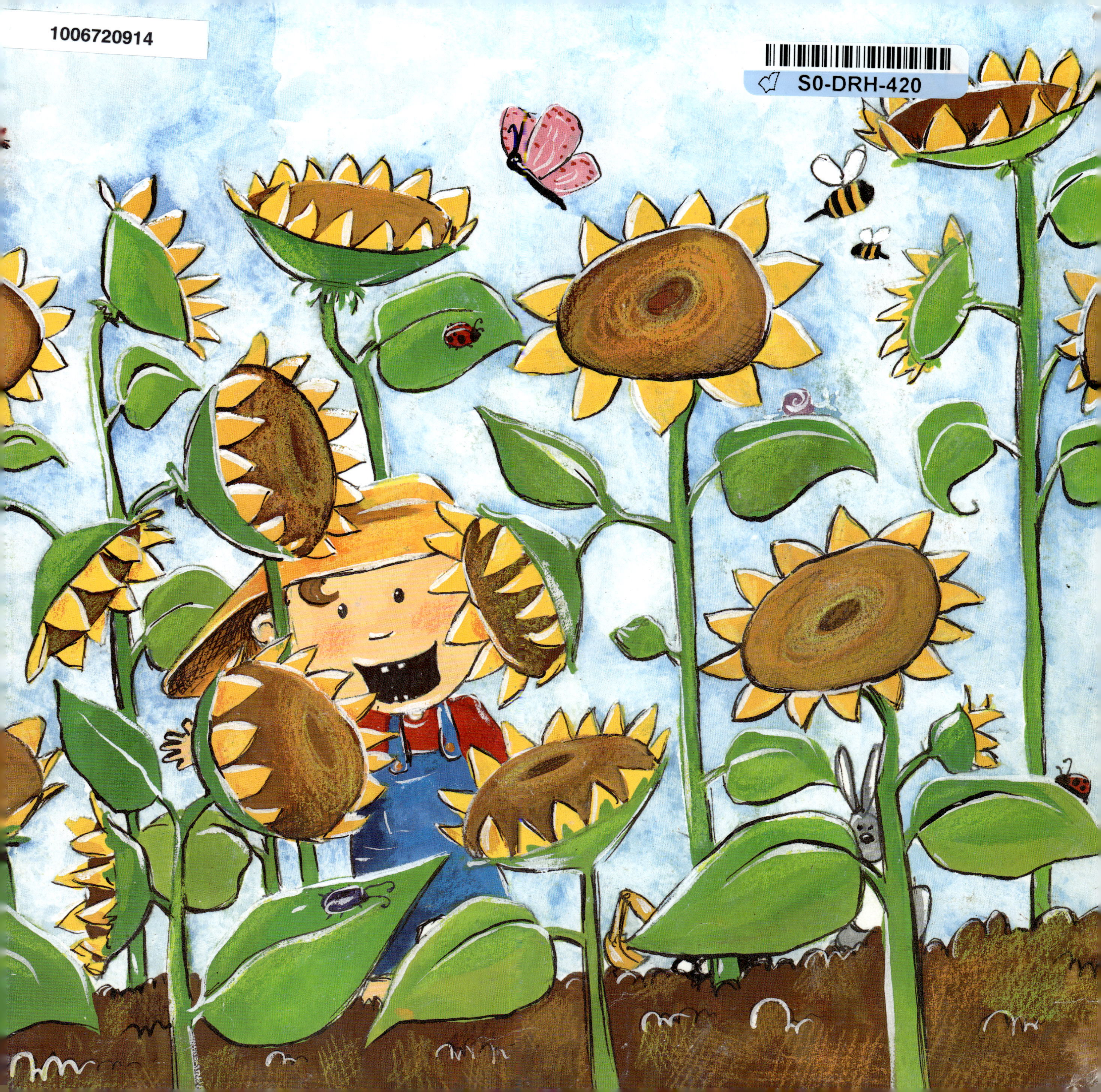

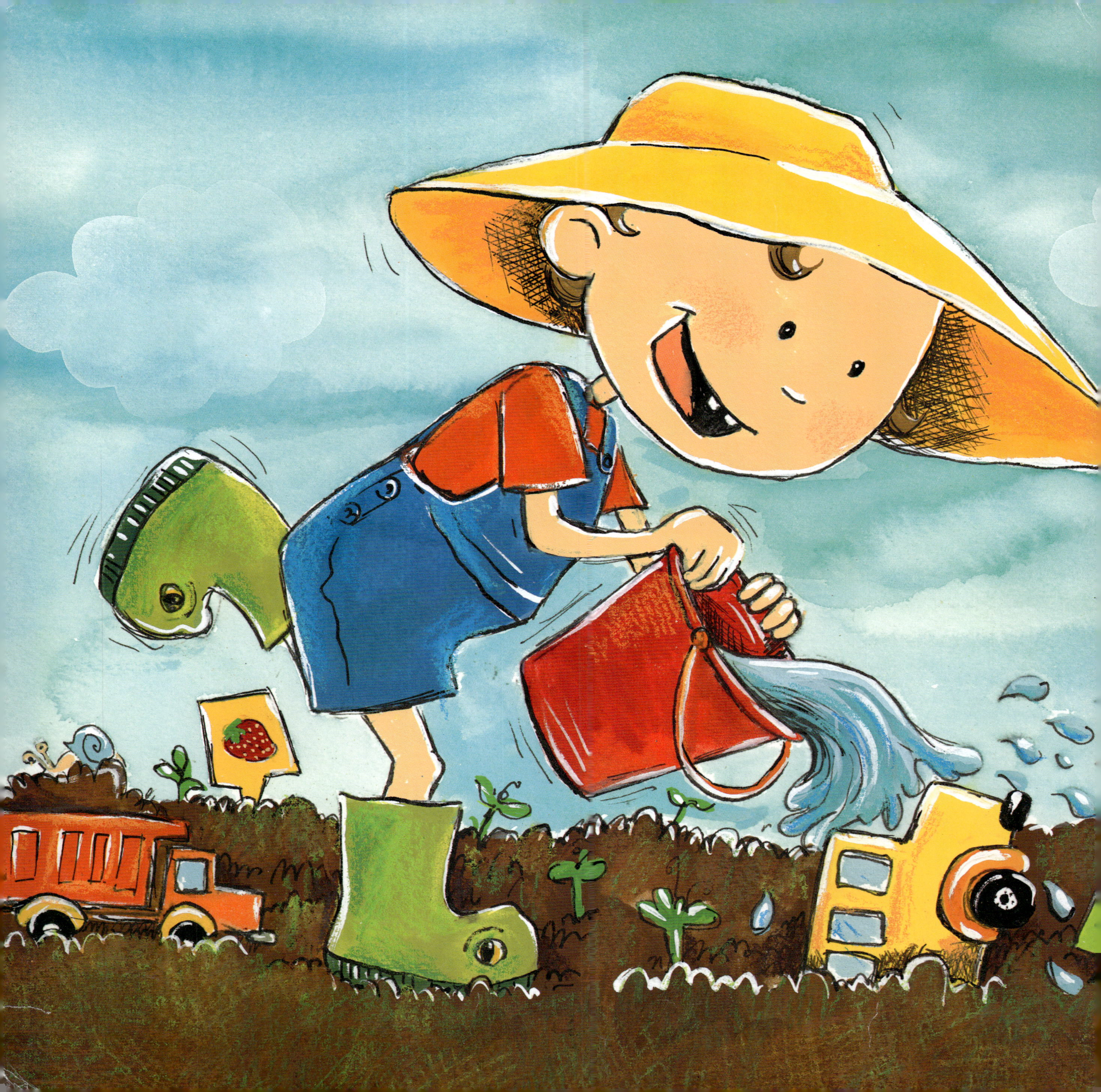

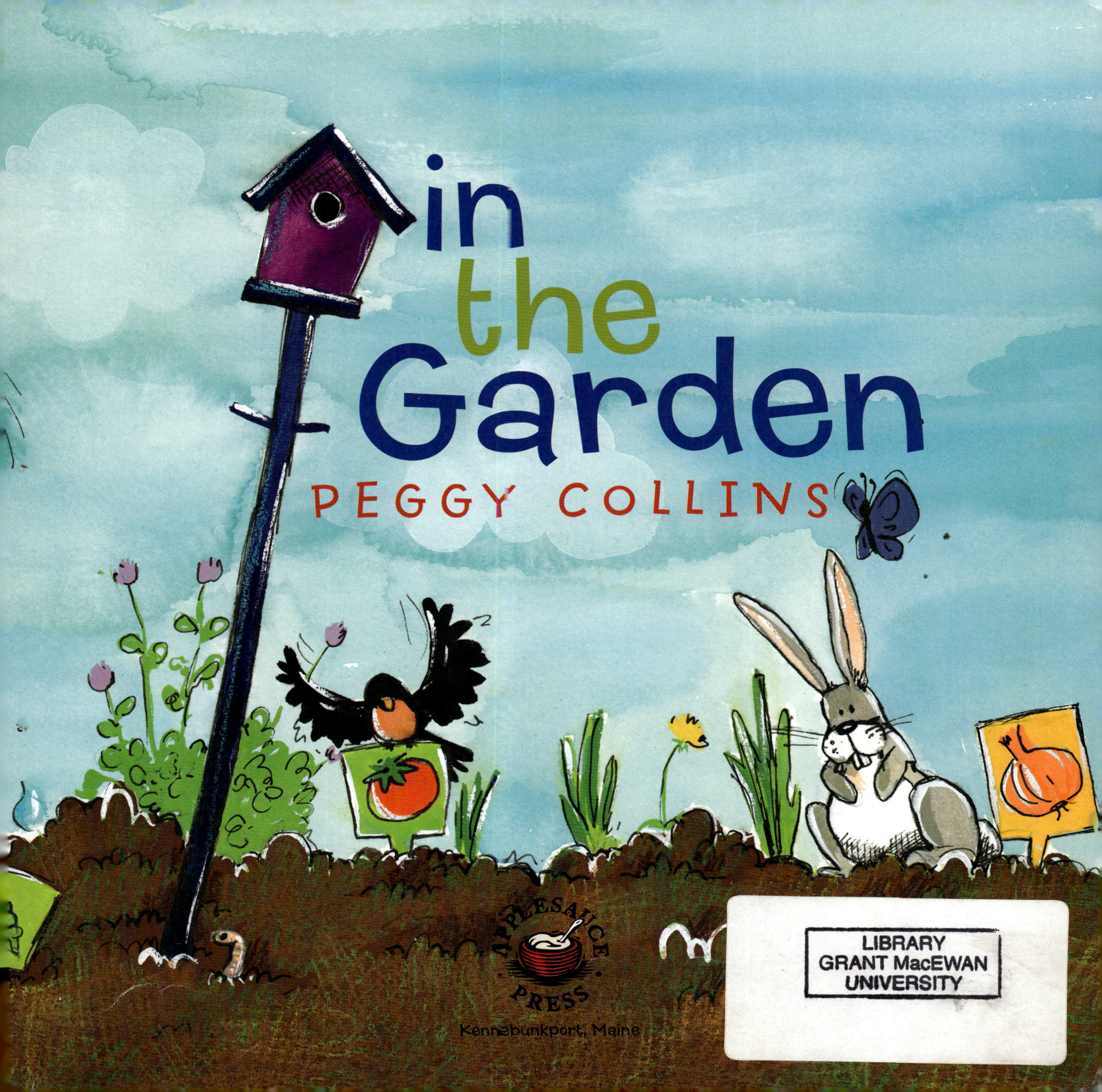

in the Garden

PEGGY COLLINS

APPLESAUCE PRESS
Kennebunkport, Maine

In the Garden
Copyright © 2009 by Peggy Collins

All rights reserved under the Pan-American and International Copyright Conventions.

No part of this book may be reproduced in whole or in part, scanned, photocopied, recorded, distributed in any printed or electronic form, or reproduced in any manner whatsoever, or by any information storage and retrieval system now known or hereafter invented, without express written permission of the publisher, except in the case of brief quotations embodied in critical articles and reviews.

The scanning, uploading, and distribution of this book via the Internet or via any other means without permission of the publisher is illegal and punishable by law. Please support authors' rights, and do not participate in or encourage piracy of copyrighted materials.

13-Digit ISBN: 978-1-60433-026-7
10-Digit ISBN: 1-60433-026-0

This book may be ordered by mail from the publisher. Please include $4.50 for postage and handling.
Please support your local bookseller first!

Books published by Cider Mill Press Book Publishers are available at special discounts for bulk purchases in the United States by corporations, institutions, and other organizations. For more information, please contact the publisher.

APPLESAUCE PRESS
is an imprint of
Cider Mill Press Book Publishers
"Where good books are ready for press"
12 Port Farm Road
Kennebunkport, Maine 04046

Visit us on the web!
www.cidermillpress.com

Illustrations created with ink, gouache, and pencil crayon
Editing and Art Direction by Elizabeth Encarnacion
Design by Peggy Collins
Typeset in Family Dog

Printed in Thailand
1 2 3 4 5 6 7 8 9 0
First Edition

for Mowat

Look at this HUGE pile of dirt in my garden...

I think I will plant some things.

I plant a truck,

a bus,

and my bulldozer.

I plant some seeds, too.

I water everything with a **BIG** watering can.

Sometimes, I make puddles on top of the seeds.

I watch
my garden.

I think maybe plants take a long time to grow.

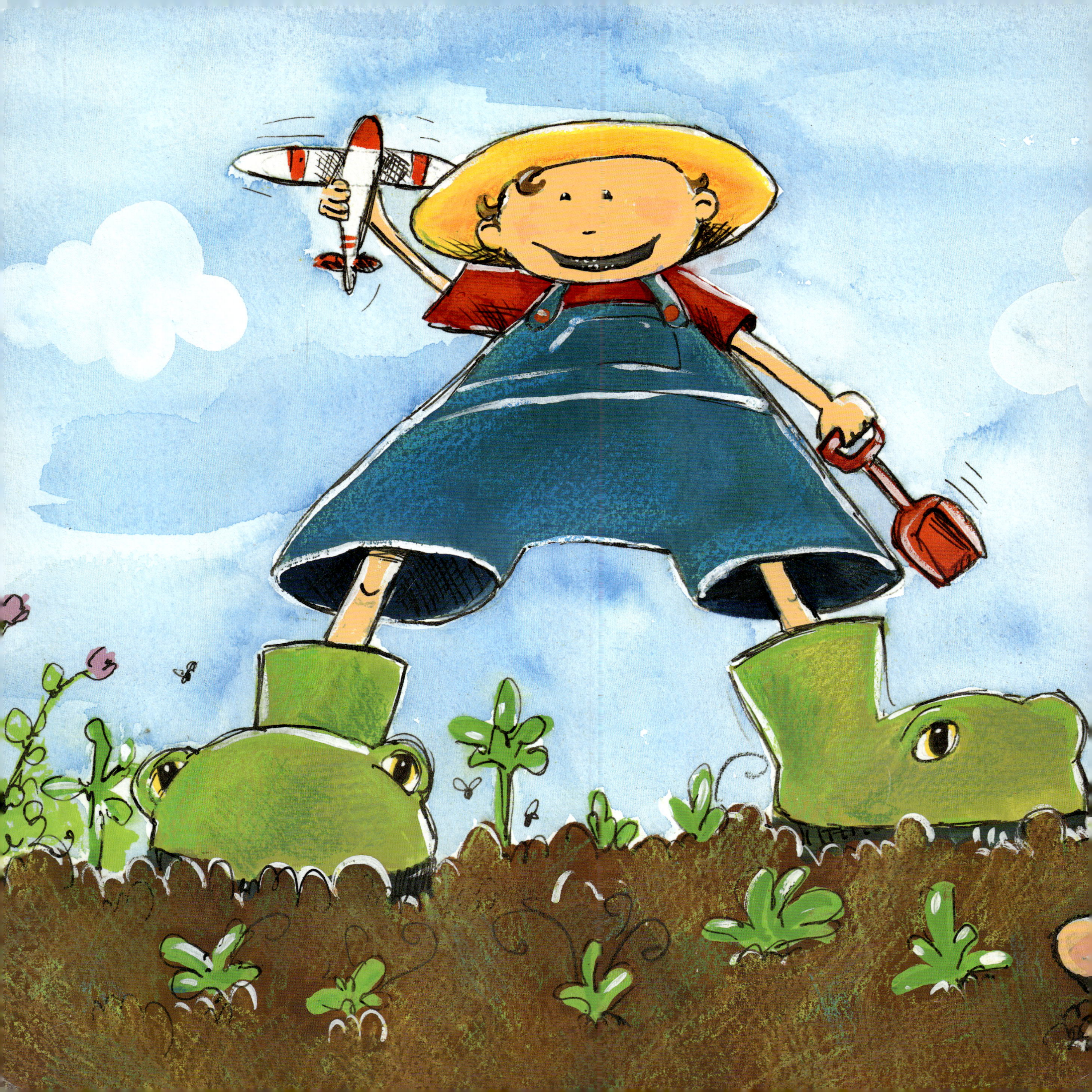

In my garden,

I am a GIANT.

Things are growing,

tiny and green.

(This giant has to be careful not to step on them!)

There are snails and slugs and ladybugs in my garden...

and hairy, hungry caterpillars, too.

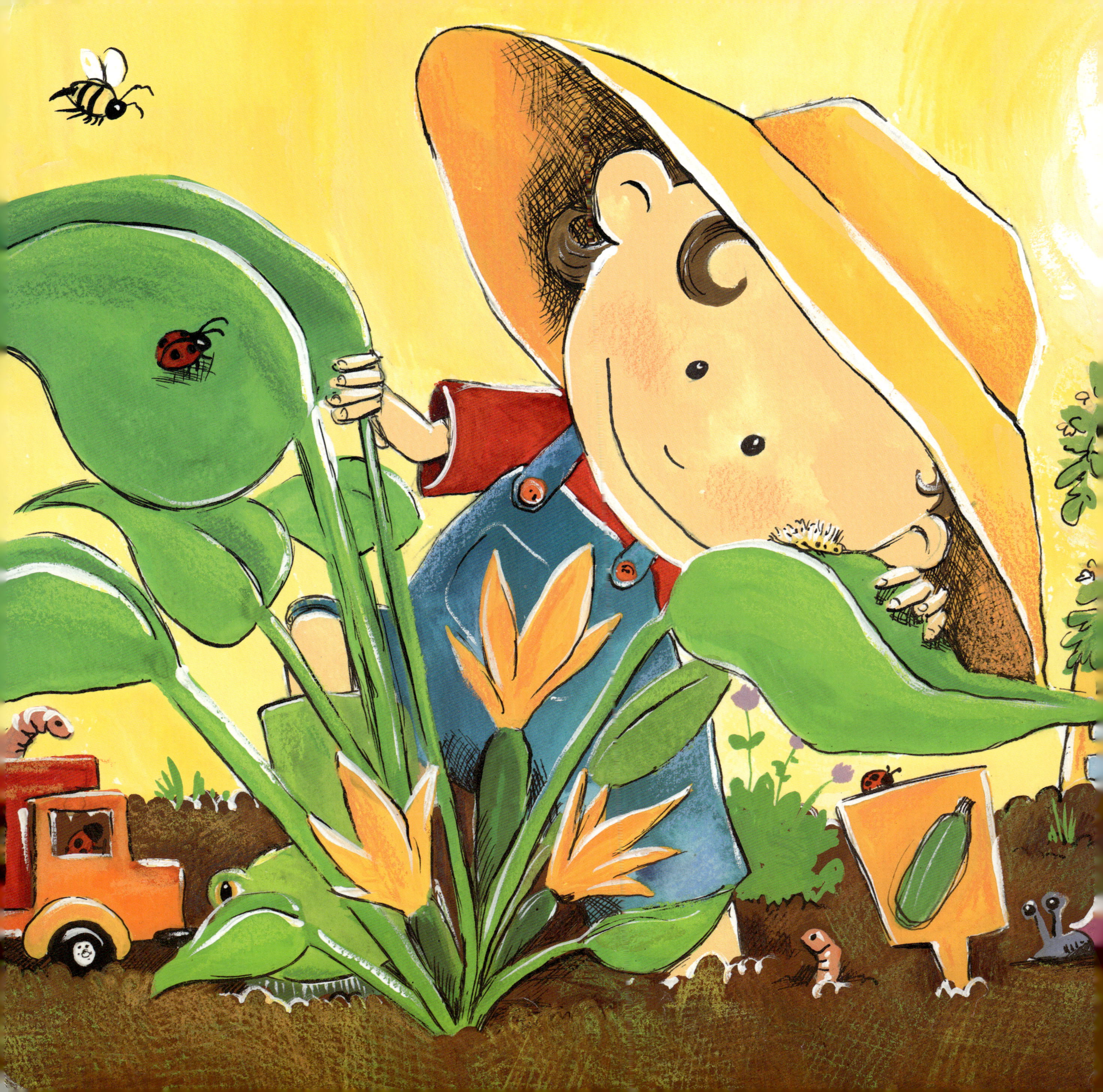

The sun shines on my garden, and flowers pop out everywhere.

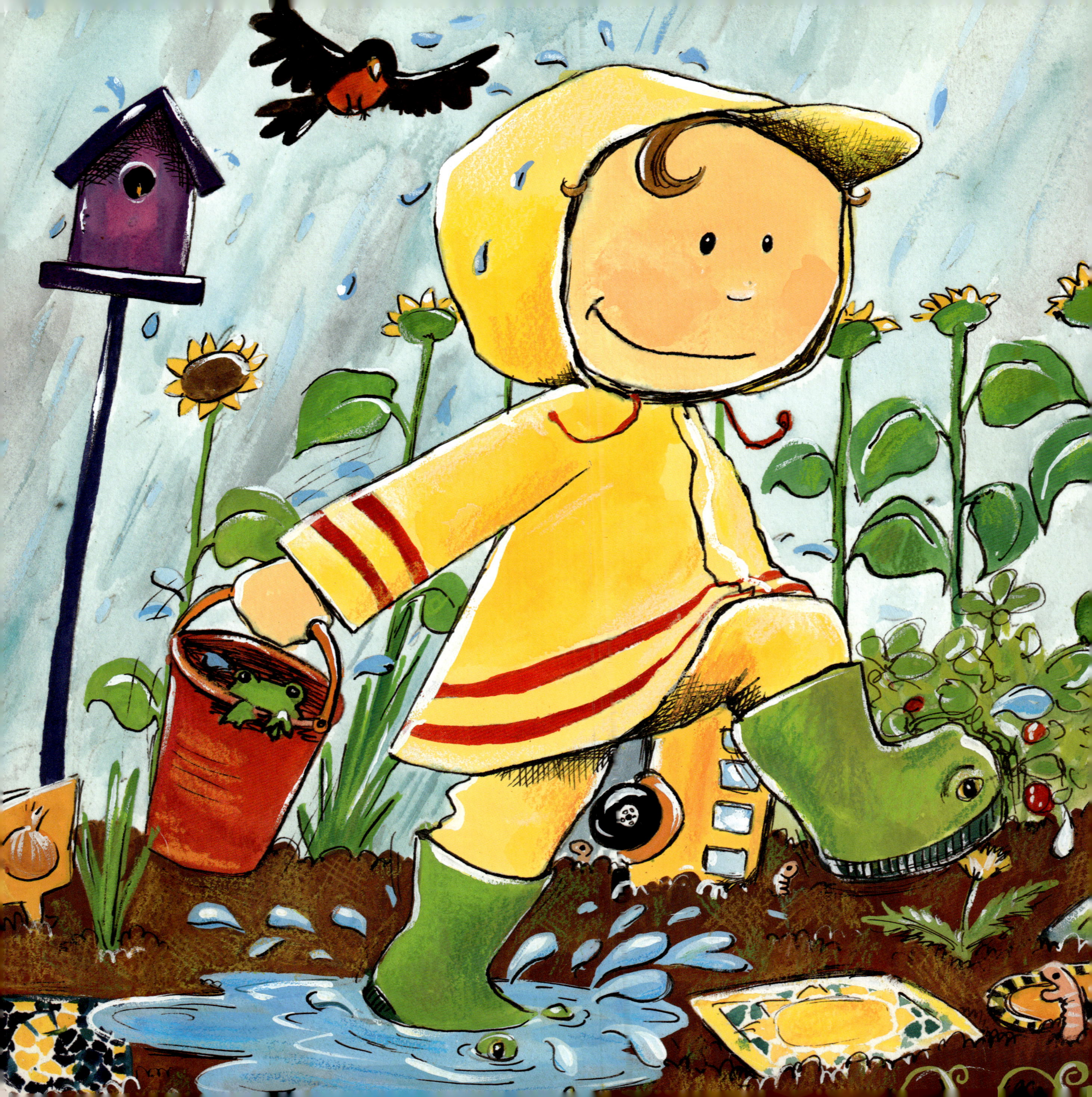

Sometimes the plants get thirsty.
When the rain falls on my garden,
they drink it right up.

In my garden,
I grow

LOTS

of

YUMMY things.

These green peas are nice
and juicy.

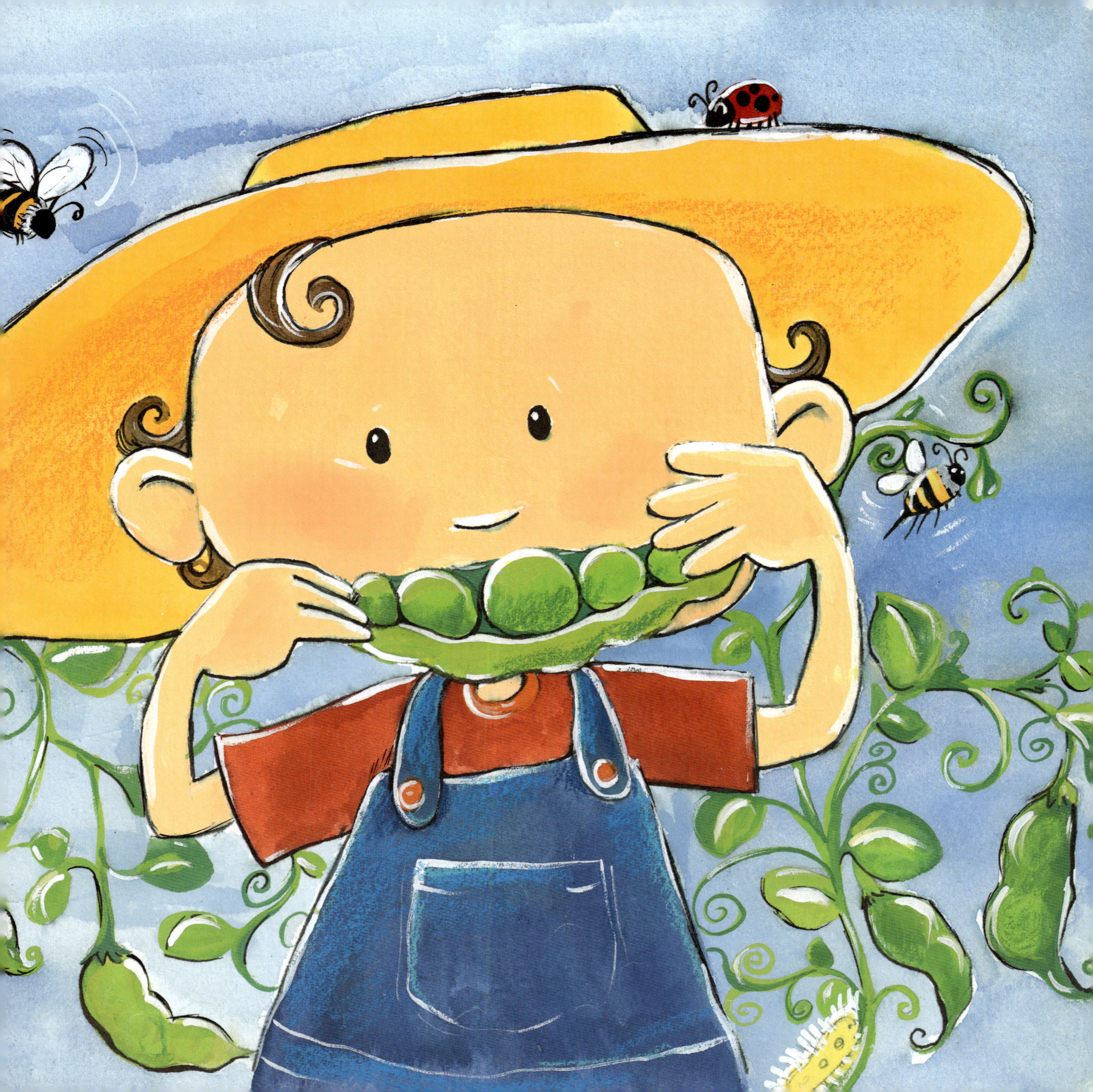

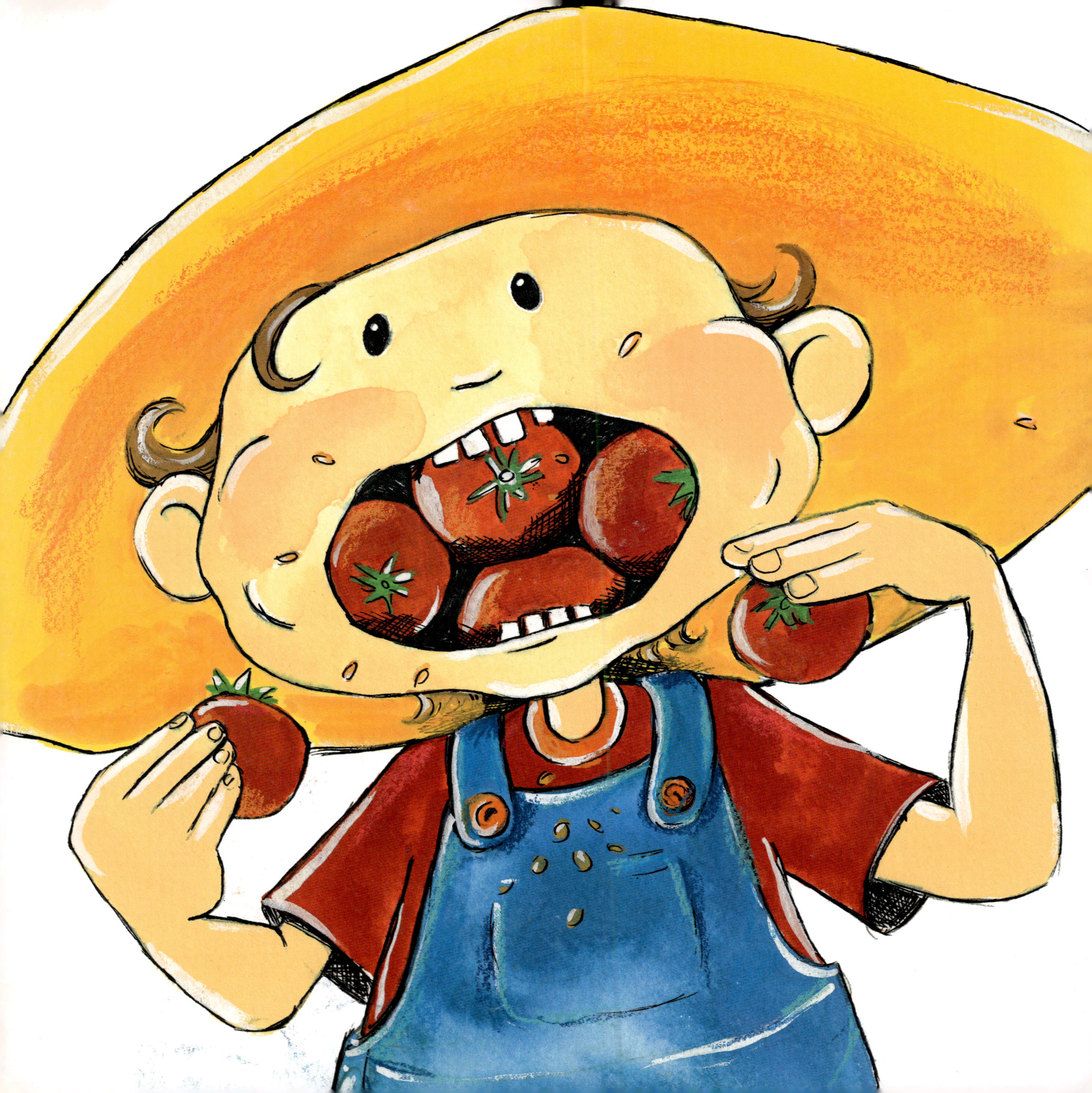

I eat mini tomatoes, and seeds squirt all over my shirt.

I squish strawberries in my mouth, and my lips turn red.

I pick some colorful, crunchy vegetables.

The bunnies also like to nibble on them.

My garden is full of butterflies, bumblebees...

and kisses.

In my garden,
the flowers have
grown into

GIANTS.

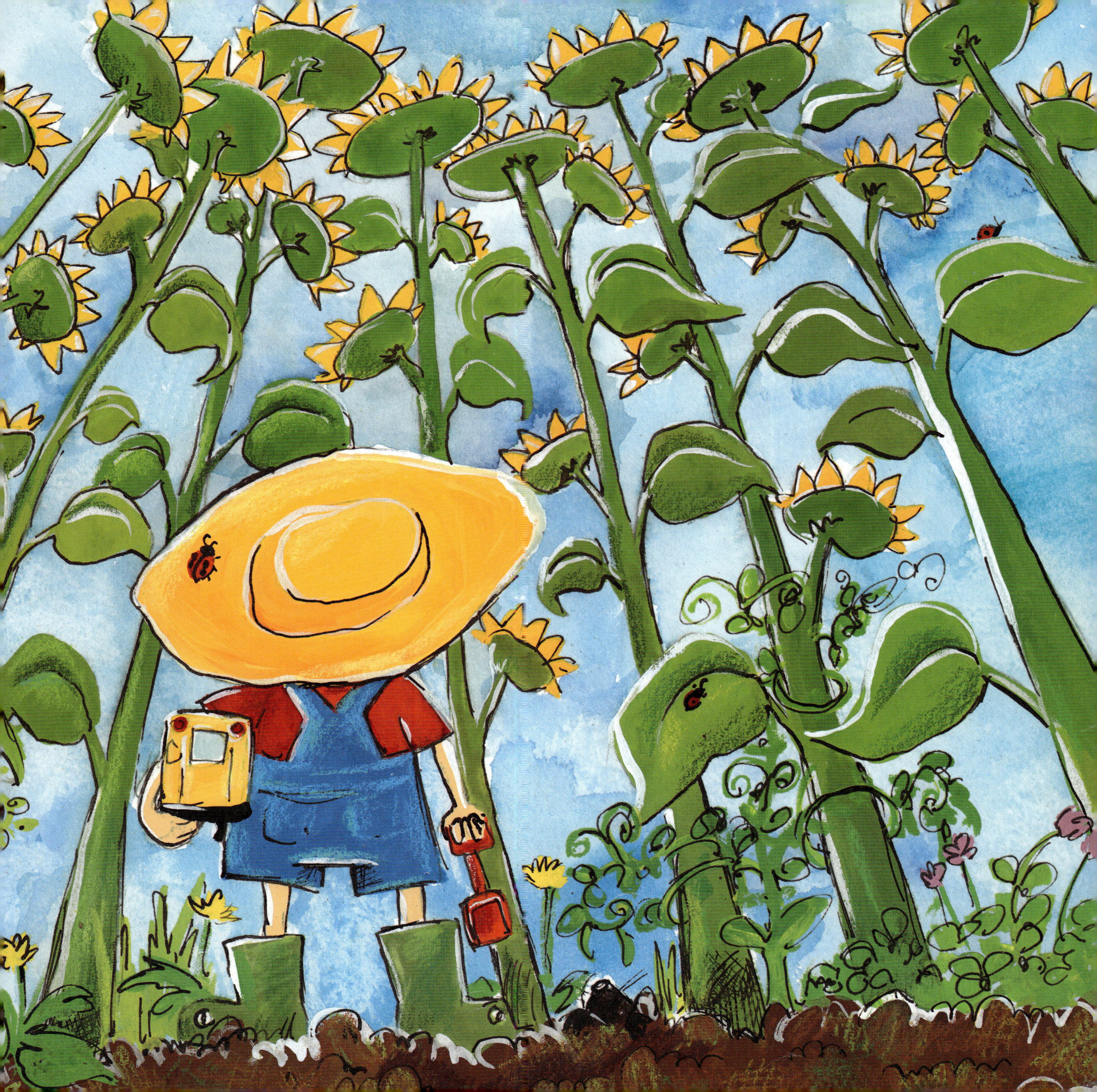

Look at my trucks! They grew so big they are driving away.

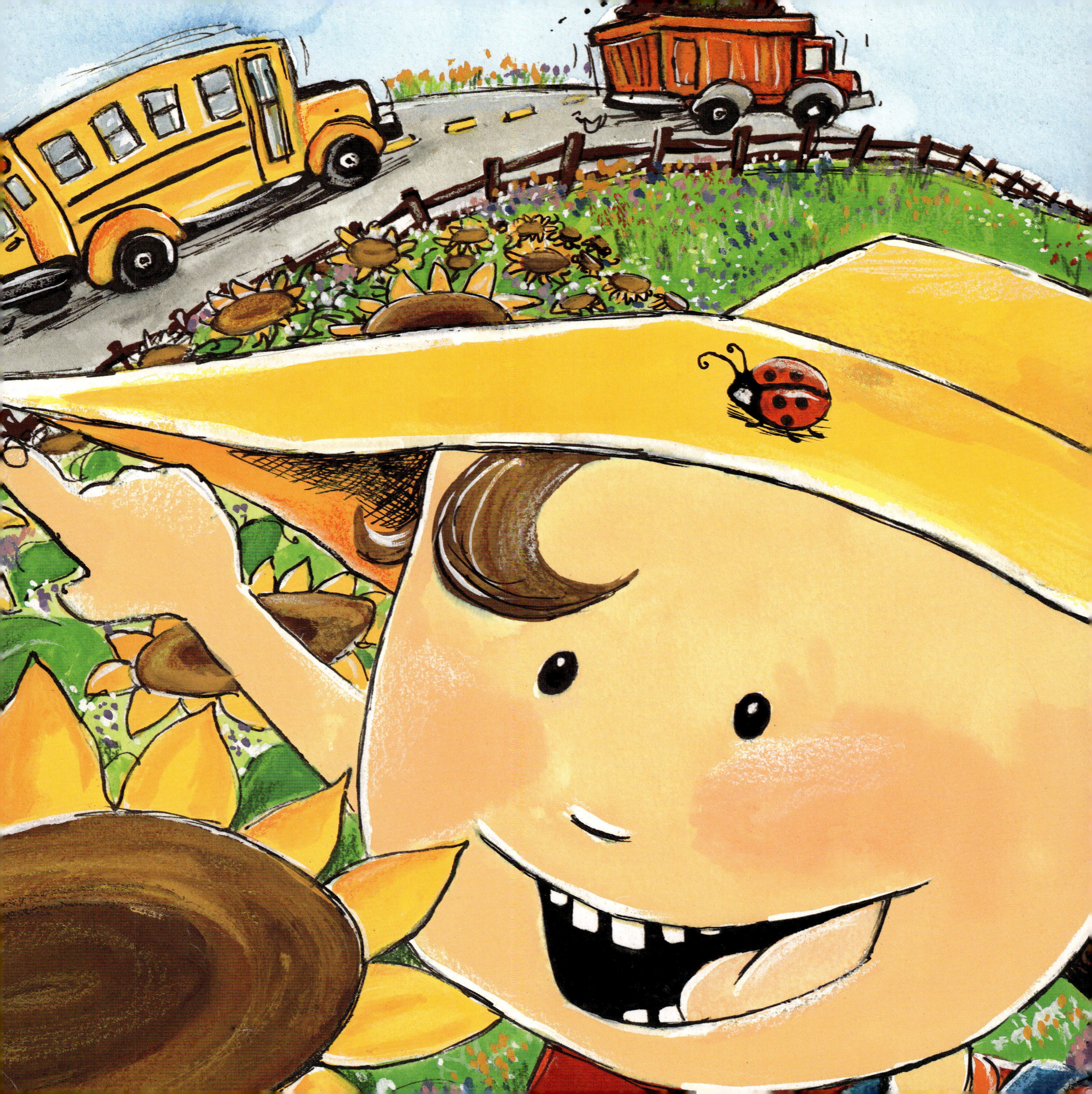

I think I grew a whole bunch, too!

About the Author

Peggy Collins has been illustrating for as long as she can remember, and still treasures the books she made in Kindergarten. Always passionate about the arts, Peggy has dabbled in all sorts of media, including sculpture, acrylic, pastel, scratchboard, and collage, though she now works primarily in gouache, pencil crayon, and ink. As a kid, she could usually be found outside playing with her sisters, inside with her nose stuck in a book, or drawing. Though this is her first book as both author and illustrator, she has created art for such books as *The End of the Dinosaurs*, *There's a Spider in the Bath*, and *Quiet Tessa*. Peggy honed her craft at Sheridan College in Oakville, Ontario, but is frequently inspired to try out new things.

Though strictly an amateur gardener, Peggy loves to muck around in her own backyard garden with her young son, who provided the inspiration for much of the text and illustration for this book. She particularly enjoyed watching him learn about food by planting seeds and eventually tasting the fresh, sun-warmed veggies straight from the ground.

Peggy would like to thank Shawn, partner, digger, and best pal, for his support through the process of digging the garden and then making this book; Mowat, who is a walking muse; her parents, sisters, Oma, Auntie Cie, and family who always trusted her to make the right choice—even when it meant art school; all of her friends who have believed in her forever; and her gardening gurus—Marg, Genny, and Jacquie, who provided the inspiration to have a garden in the first place.

Please visit Peggy's website at www.peggycollinsillustration.com

> "Let go of any ideas you might have for a perfect garden.
> Let the seeds fall where they may.
> If your child plants them—leave them, nurture them,
> and treat them with reverence." —M. B.

About Applesauce Press

What kid doesn't love Applesauce!

Applesauce Press was created to press out the best children's books found anywhere. Like our parent company, Cider Mill Press Book Publishers, we strive to bring fine reading, information, and entertainment to kids of all ages. Between the covers of our creatively crafted books, you'll find beautiful designs, creative formats, and most of all, kid-friendly information on a variety of topics. Our Cider Mill bears fruit twice a year, publishing a new crop of titles each spring and fall.

"Where Good Books are Ready for Press"

Visit us on the web at
www.cidermillpress.com
or write to us at
12 Port Farm Road
Kennebunkport, Maine 04046

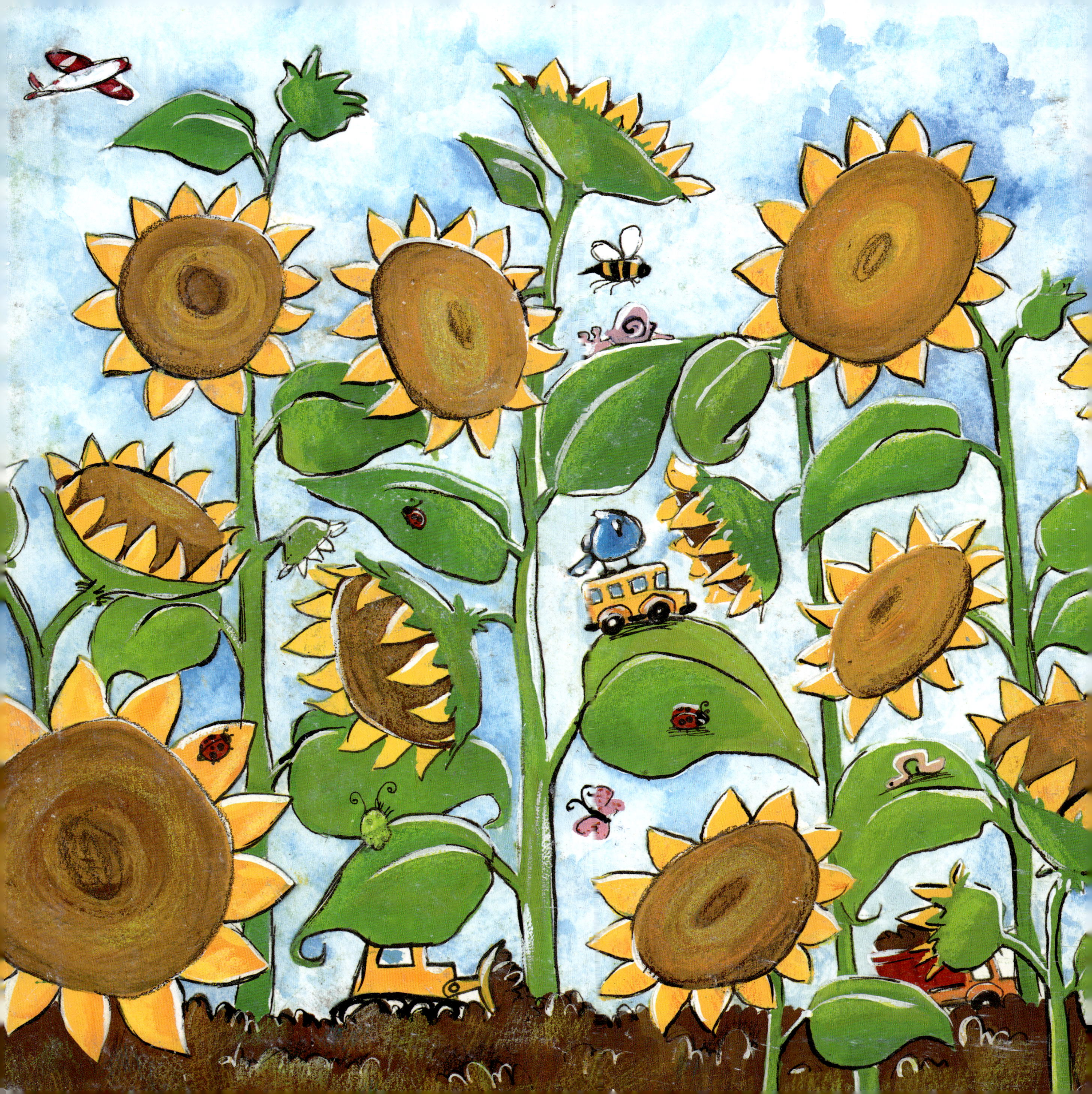